This book belongs to:

Have a Grr-Great day!
Tim Ostermey
10/7/14

_____ Ana _____

_____

MW01065694

Titus & Tiana

Lesson for Baby Tigers

by Master Photographer
Tim Ostermeyer

Titus and Tiana were so comfortable
in their nice tiger den.
Tiana suddenly noticed that
their sister, named Albany, was missing.
They began to feel bad about
making fun of her for being different.
"Is it possible that she ran away because
we made fun of her?"
Titus asked.

Titus ran out of the den to see if
he could locate his sister.
Titus felt bad.
"We should not have laughed at
her for being different,"
Titus sighed.

Titus and Tiana
looked in the valley to see if
Albany had run down the mountain.
It looks like Albany has
run away.

Tiana shouted,
"Albany, where are you?"
But still, there was no answe

Tiana then gave a blank stare, because she was so concerned for her little sister. "We should never have made fun of her. We can now blame ourselves for her disappearance."

Mother was very concerned about her missing cub.
"I wish that Titus & Tiana had not bullied her," mom thought to herself.

Mother really missed Albany, and she looked for her with her whole heart.

She really wished that her three cubs got along.

Then Albany would not be missing.

Mother climbed on a rock to see if she could locate her precious cub.

Mother searched carefully in the tall grass for her little cub.

Was her baby tiger hidden in this tall grass somewhere?

Did you know that Tigers ...

Have more than 100 stripes

Have a unique stripe pattern, with no 2 tigers alike

Are an endangered species

Are hunted for fur and other body parts used for medicine

Are the largest cats, weighing up to 720 lb

Front paws are larger than rear paws, to attack better

Are 6 feet long with a 3 foot tail

Have a roar heard 2 miles away

Are born with blue eyes that turn to gold later

Mother looked for Albany
by the small pond,
but she is not found here.

Did you know
that Jaguars ...

Are solitary, they
live and hunt alone

Are great swimmers

Weight up to 250 lb

Defend a territory
of 20 to 50 miles
which may include
1 or 2 females

Are an endangered
species

Hunt mainly at night

Have rosette circles
with spots inside

Are more muscular
with shorter legs and
tails than the cheetah

Can only run 27 mph
Slower than most
animals

Are third largest
cat

The jaguar was calling out
to the tiger cub,
but Albany
did not respond.

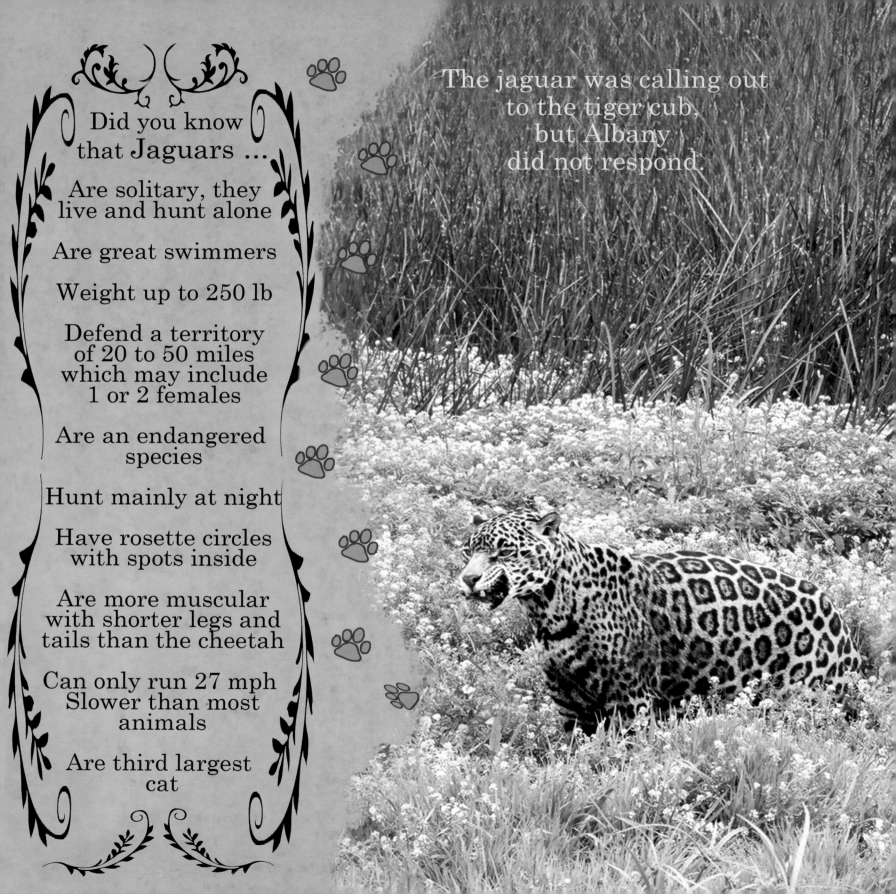

The jaguar was not happy that the baby tiger was still missing.
"I'll go looking on the other side of the lake," he told the mother tiger.

"Maybe the tiger cub can hear my roaring,
or because of my hunger, hear my stomach growling."

The jaguar kept swimming,
being sure to show his teeth
to scare away other dangerous animals
in the water.

It also allowed him to breath
while swimming, which
he found to be
very helpful.

Mother cried out to her little cub,
"Where are you baby?"

But then she went to sleep
without her baby.

The lion ran down from the mountains
to see if the tiger cub
was hiding in the valley.

The lion walked down
to the beach to see if the
tiger cub went swimming.

"The water looks so nice,
maybe I should go swimming,"
says the lion.

The lion remembered
what he was there for,
to find the tiger cub,
so he looked to his right.

The lion glanced to his left.
He looked all over the sandy beach
for the little tiger cub,
as the waves crashed
onto the beach.

Did you know
that Lions ...

If males, are called
lions or toms

If females, are called
she-lions or lionesses

Are the second biggest cat
in the world,
weighing up to 530 lb

Live in groups called
"prides"

Sleep up to
20 hours a day

Have one dominant
male lion in the pride
who acts like a king
and guards the many
lionesses and cubs

Are the only member
of the cat family with
a mane and tuft
(ball at end of tail)

Run 50 mph, faster
than a fox, wolf,
or bear

The wind was blowing hard.
The hot weather was
also bothering the lion.
He spent so much time
looking over the entire beach,
that the lion became tired.

"Keep looking, keep looking,"
he kept telling himself.

The lion is sad that he did not find the cub, that he drops his head in disappointment.

"Maybe I will find Albany later," he thinks as he trys to cheer himself.

Splish, splash, she is taking a bath!

Not really. Mother has a mean look in her eye,
as she runs through the fields looking for her daughter.

She is angry that her baby tiger did not listen to her rule
about staying close to the family.

Mother ran up and down the fields
hoping to alert Albany
with her splashing sounds.
"Is is possible that she fell asleep in the field?"
she thought.

Albany,
"Where are you baby?"
Mother cries out.

Did you know that Black Leopards ...

Are also called black panthers

Number 50,000 in the world

Get their black color from "melanin" in their skin and hair

Are found in a litter of regular-colored leopards

Hunt at night, when they cannot be seen

Are not fussy eaters; they will eat anything

Protect their territory of 12 square miles

The black leopard looked for the cub in the green grass. "I hope that we find her soon," he growled.

Did you know
that Ocelots ...

Live in forests
and brushy areas

Are about twice the
size of a house cat

Swim well

Eat rabbits,
rodents, iguanas,
fish, and frogs

Run 38 mph

Do not have teeth
appropriate for
chewing so they
tear food and
swallow it
hole

The ocelot with
mostly dots
was looking
for a tiger
cub with
stripes.

The ocelot peaked through
a hole in the cave.
"Peek a boo,
are you in here,
little tiger cub?"

The lioness gave a sad look, because she could not find the tiger cub. She prowled the hillside as she continued to look for Albany.

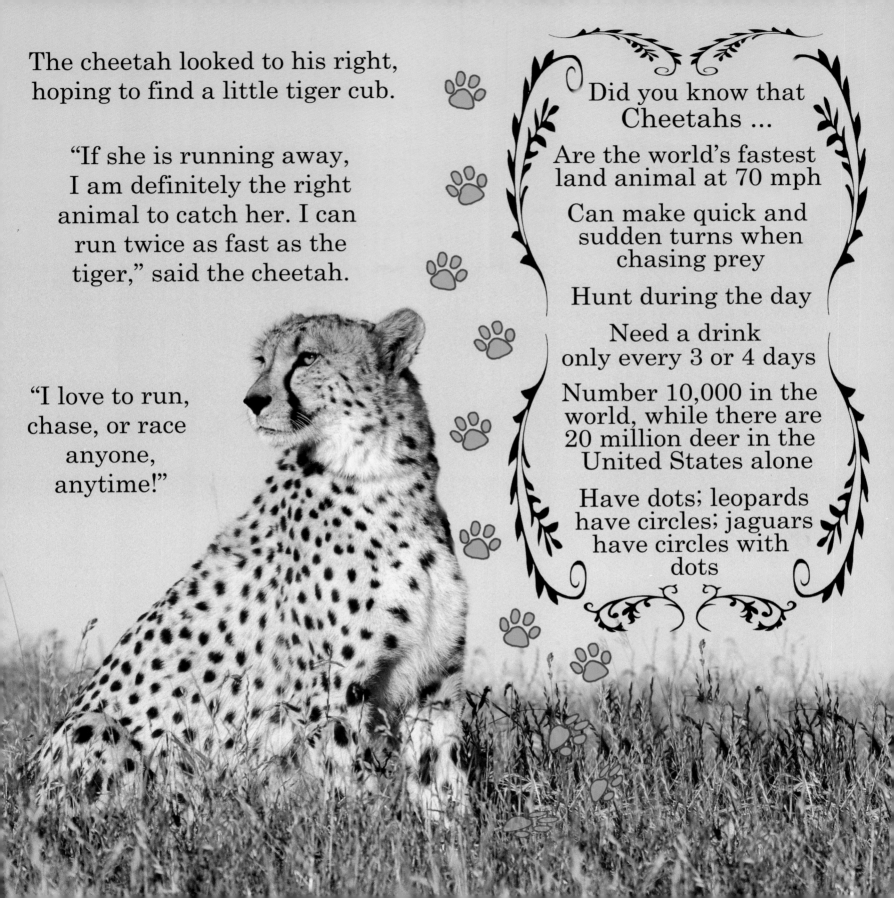

The cheetah looked to his right, hoping to find a little tiger cub.

"If she is running away, I am definitely the right animal to catch her. I can run twice as fast as the tiger," said the cheetah.

"I love to run, chase, or race anyone, anytime!"

Did you know that Cheetahs ...

Are the world's fastest land animal at 70 mph

Can make quick and sudden turns when chasing prey

Hunt during the day

Need a drink only every 3 or 4 days

Number 10,000 in the world, while there are 20 million deer in the United States alone

Have dots; leopards have circles; jaguars have circles with dots

The cheetah left quickly.

He took off so fast that he almost left his spots behind.

The cheetah ran to the other side of the field to see if Albany was lost there.

The cheetah reached his
top speed of 70 mph.
He enjoys being the fastest land animal in the world.

In comparison, the fastest man on earth can only run 27 mph.
The cheetah is 2.5 times faster.

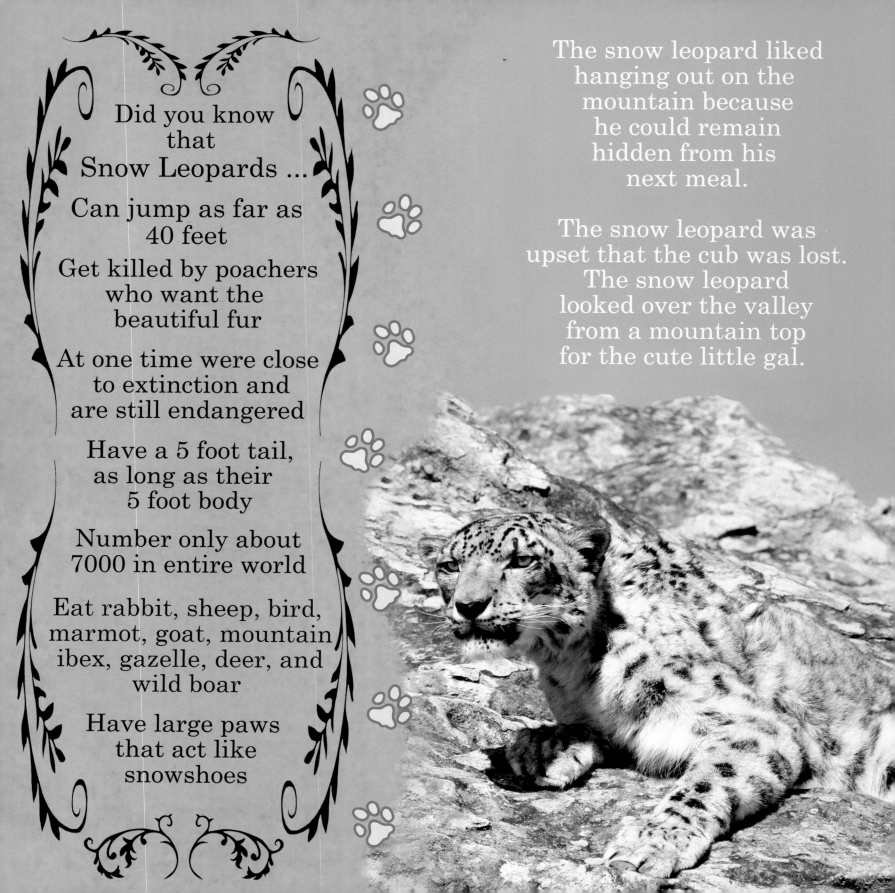

Did you know
that
Snow Leopards ...

Can jump as far as
40 feet

Get killed by poachers
who want the
beautiful fur

At one time were close
to extinction and
are still endangered

Have a 5 foot tail,
as long as their
5 foot body

Number only about
7000 in entire world

Eat rabbit, sheep, bird,
marmot, goat, mountain
ibex, gazelle, deer, and
wild boar

Have large paws
that act like
snowshoes

The snow leopard liked
hanging out on the
mountain because
he could remain
hidden from his
next meal.

The snow leopard was
upset that the cub was lost.
The snow leopard
looked over the valley
from a mountain top
for the cute little gal.

The snow leopard worked so hard looking,
that he decided to take a nap.

Mom missed her little cub so badly.
She looked over a tree branch in hopes of
finding her hiding from enemies.

Mom was hoping to say,
"Peak a boo, I see you!

The little tiger cub was not here either.

Did you know that Leopards ...

Are so strong that they drag their large prey up into trees

Eat large animals like gazelle, impala, deer, and wildebeest

Also eat small animals like monkeys, rats, and birds

Are strong swimmers

Eat fish and crabs when in the water

Number 50,000 in the world

Kill prey mostly at night

Can see and hear very well

Can run 40 mph

Have long tails 3 feet long

"So many people confuse me with two other wild cats. It is really quite simple," said the leopard.

"I am a leopard and have circles, cheetahs have dots, and jaguars have dots in circles."

The leopard is good
at climbing trees.
He climbs high to
carefully looks for Albany
from this tall vantage point.

Time passed on, and their appearance changed.

Now they really worried about Albany.
Was she well fed or would she look smaller for lack of food?

What detail of the tigers have changed?
Sure they are bigger, but compare Titus & Tiana
now to the beginning of this book.
The observant child may qualify as
a future FBI agent.

Titus began thinking. "The jaguar looked in the lake. The lion looked on the beach. The black leopard looked in the green fields. The ocelot looked in the cave. The leopard looked in the trees."

"Where else could we possibly look to find my sister."

Tiana snuggled up to her mother.
"Look far in the distance.
Is that Albany that we see out there?"
Tiana asks.

The tiger's roar can only be heard 2 miles,
and Albany is just over 2 miles away.
"I can roar louder than that." says the jaguar.
The jaguar yells out as loud as he can,
"Albany, can you hear me?"

Sure enough, far in the distance was a sad and lost little tiger cub named Albany. Albany could hear the jaguar calling in the distance. Albany was an albino tiger cub, all white from birth, different from everyone else. Albany was lost for months, and by this time, she was cold, hungry, and under-sized for not getting enough food.

She was very pleased to hear the jaguar growling. Albany did not know that she would be rescued that night because Tiana and her mother could see her white fur from a distance in the dark. Her difference and uniqueness became her very best feature, and it saved her life.

By morning, Albany was telling Titus and Tiana all about her adventures. "It was exciting at first, but then I got really scared. I missed my family and got really hungry."

"This is a good lesson for every tiger cub and for every boy and girl."

"Always stay close to your parents, brother, and sister and you will never get lost."

"Thanks for finding me!" Albany shouted out as she smiled.

Albany then remembered back three months ago,
when she was safe in the den with Tiana and Titus.
"It was so warm and comfortable with my family.
I will never run away from home again!" Albany declared.

Titus and Tiana agreed that they
would never tease her ever again.
They would never make fun of her for being different.
They would now consider her to be very special,
for being so wonderfully unique.

Wild Cat Jokes

1) What lion never moves? A dandelion
2) What is the silliest name to give a tiger? Spot
3) What do you call a show with some lions? The mane event
4) What cat should you never play cards with ? A cheetah
5) Did you hear about the lion show? It was a roaring success
6) Who came out alive of the tiger den? The tiger
7) What is tan with red spots? A cheetah with measles
8) When is a lion not a lion? When he turns into a cage
9) Why don't cheetahs escape from zoos?
   They are too easily spotted
10) What do you get when a tiger meets a polar bear? Frostbite
11) What do tigers and sergeants have in common? Stripes
12) Difference between tiger and lion? Tiger has mane part missing
13) What do you do when a leopard sleeps in your room?
    Sleep in another room
14) How do you take the tiger's temperature? Very carefully

The Author is So Appreciative of the Scenic Beauty & Gorgeous Wildlife That He Has Witnessed in His Travels

Thanks to Fiona Pinsker
for the jokes on the joke page

These are the cutest baby animals on earth, Call 1-972-542-7065 to order the whole set.
(Gorgeous baby wildlife photos, Up to 220 facts per book, fun story line, moral messages)

Baby Foxes	Baby Penguins	Baby Tigers	Baby Polar Bears	Baby Snow Monkeys	Baby Ducks	Bald Eagle	Baby Kangaroos
					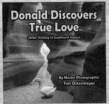		
Sharing	Exploring	Bullying	Going After Dreams	Planning	Finding True Love	Applying the Word	Fear vs Confidence

Copyright 2012 Tim Ostermeyer - All Rights Reserved

No part of this book may be reproduced in any manner without the publisher's
expressed written consent, except in the case of brief
excerpts in critical reviews and articles.
Inquiries about this book should be addressed to:

Published by Fun Adventure Wildlife Books

1813 Country Brook Lane
Allen, Texas 75002
1-972-542-7065
www.FunAdventureWildlifeBooks.com
www.ostermeyer-photography.com

Library of Congress Catalog Data on File with Publisher
ISBN: 978-0-9794228-6-7

Printed and Bound in Canada (Friesens of Altona, Manitoba)

Storyline, Photography, Graphic Art, and Cover Design by Tim Ostermeyer
Words by Tim Ostermeyer